USBORNE FIRST R[...]
Level Three

USBORNE FIRST READING

Monkeys

Sarah Courtauld
illustrated by
Daniel Howarth

USB[...]

The Mouse's Wedding

[...]nnon
Illustrated by Frank Endersby

The Peach Boy

Retold by
Alex Frith
Illustrated by
Kelly Murphy

The Castle That Jack Built

Lesley Sims
Illustrated by
Mike Gordon

Noah's Ark

Retold by Kate Davies

Illustrated by John Joven

Reading consultant: Alison Kelly
Roehampton University

Long, long ago, God
made the world.

He loved almost
everything in it.

But he didn't like
the people.

They were cruel and cross.

They lied and cheated.

And they didn't listen
to God.

There was one good man,
named Noah.

He worked
hard and loved God.

God went to see him.

"I'm going to flood the
Earth," said God.

"I'll wash the bad
people away."

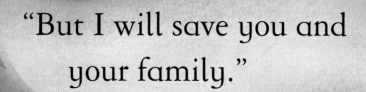

"But I will save you and your family."

God told Noah to build
an ark.

"The ark will float and
keep you safe," he said.

10

So Noah got to work.
His whole family helped.

They worked for weeks
and weeks.

At last,
the ark was finished.

13

Noah looked up
at the ark.

It was so tall,
he couldn't see the top.

"Don't get in yet," said God. "I want to save the animals, too."

Just then, Noah heard a rumbling noise.

Hundreds of animals were rushing to the ark.

Eagles swooped...

horses galloped...

and snakes slithered in.

Two by two,
bees buzzed on
board

and huge elephants
squeezed through the door.

18

Noah packed plenty
of food and drink.

Then he climbed in, too.

20

God shut the door tight.

They waited... and
waited. A week went by.

Splish! Raindrops started splashing from the sky.

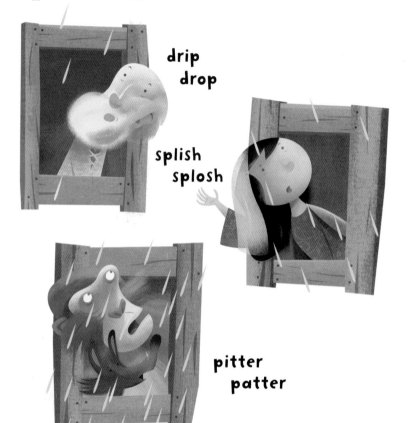

drip
drop

splish
splosh

pitter
patter

Soon the rain drummed loudly on the roof.

It rained non-stop
for forty days...

...and forty nights.

The rain fell until it covered the tallest mountain.

The ark floated on a
brand new sea.

At last, the sun came out.

Noah looked
outside.

All he could
see was water.

Noah sent a raven to
look for dry land.

The raven looked for days
and days.

It couldn't find land
anywhere.

Noah sent out a dove.

The dove looked for days
and days.

Then it flew back with an
olive leaf.

31

"Trees must be growing somewhere!" said Noah.

But where's the land?

32

He sent the dove to look
again.

He waited... and waited... but the dove didn't come back.

Noah looked out of
the ark.

Hooray!

He could see the tops of
the mountains again.

Slowly, the water
went away.

When the land was dry,
Noah opened the ark.

The elephants squeezed
through the door. The bees
buzzed into the fresh air.

The snakes slithered out.

The horses galloped away.

And the eagles
soared high into the sky.

Noah and his
family went outside,
blinking in the sun.

"Go to every corner of the world and have families," God told the animals.

The animals set out to find new homes.

Noah and his family
picked a perfect spot
for their new house.

"Thank you for saving us,
God," said Noah.

God made a rainbow
in the sky.

"I promise never to
flood the world again,"
said God.

45

About Noah's Ark

Noah's Ark is one of the best-known Bible stories. It appears in Genesis, the first book of the Bible, but there are lots of different stories about a huge flood from ancient times. Flood stories are told in Christianity, Islam and Judaism.

Consultant: Dr Katharine Dell,
University of Cambridge
Designed by Caroline Spatz
Series editor: Lesley Sims
Series designer: Russell Punter

First published in 2011 by Usborne Publishing Ltd.,
Usborne House, 83-85 Saffron Hill, London EC1N 8RT, England.
www.usborne.com Copyright © 2011 Usborne Publishing Ltd.

USBORNE FIRST READING
Level Four

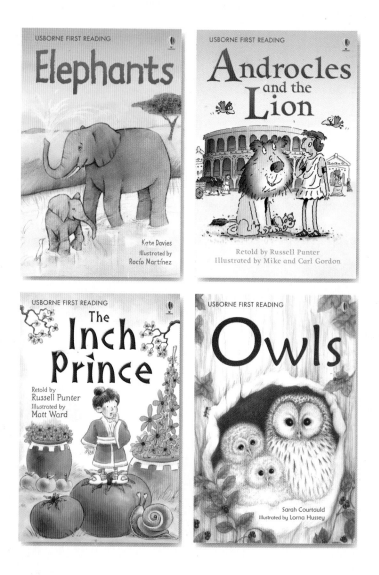